Cow's ding dong bell

Written by Jillian Harker
Illustrated by Simon Abbott

PaRragon

Bath · New York · Singapore · Hong Kong · Cologne · Delhi · Melbourne

The animals at Goosefeather Farm were not in a good mood.

Goat was grumpy. Cat was cross. The sheep were all short-tempered. And Hen was hopping mad!

But there was one animal who didn't seem to notice…

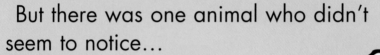

Cow strolled down the lane to the dairy with a big grin on her face.

Ding-dong! Ding-dong!

With every step, the big bell round her neck clanged out its tune. Cow loved her bell. She was so proud of it that she jiggled her head as she walked, just to make it ring louder!

Round the corner, Cow noticed Horse.
He didn't look happy.

"Good morning, Horse," said Cow
cheerfully. "How are you today?"

"I've got a headache," moaned Horse.
"It's very noisy round here!"

"Really?" said Cow. "I hadn't noticed."
And she strolled on, her big bell ringing
as she went.

In the farmyard, Rooster glared at Cow as she came into the yard.

"I got up early for nothing," he squawked. "I crowed and crowed, but no-one heard me – someone was making *so much* noise!"

"Oh!" said Cow, in surprise. "I wonder who that could have been?" And she swung her head from side to side, to start her bell ringing again.

Then Cow saw Cat. "I've been calling my kittens for hours and none of them have come home. I'm not surprised, with someone making all that racket!" meowed Cat.

"How thoughtless!" exclaimed Cow. She shook her head and the bell rang louder!

"You should do something about it," she smiled, as she walked off.

Hen came rushing across the yard.

"I've really had enough of this!" she clucked.
"I can't hear myself think. Cow! Come here!"

Cow turned round.

"Is there a problem?" she asked.

"YES!" yelled all the animals together. **"You and your bell!"**

Cow was shocked. "What *do* you mean?"

"That bell! It's driving us crazy!" they cried, angrily. "You're keeping us awake all night and we're *really* tired of it!"

"Oh!" said Cow.
"If that's how you feel,
I'd better go where you
can't hear it."

And she walked away,
shaking her head sadly.

Ding!

Ding!

Ding!

That evening, the animals settled down in the barn for the night.

"My headache's gone," smiled Horse.

"I shall wake you with an especially fine song tomorrow," crowed Rooster.

Cat snuggled all her kittens on the warm straw. Very soon, everyone was fast asleep.

A little later, Horse woke up. At first, he couldn't work out what was wrong. It was dark and he was sure he hadn't been asleep for long. Then he knew what it was – smoke!

"Fire! Fire!" he neighed.

The other animals woke up and hurried towards the barn door.

But when they got there, they found it was shut tight!

Out in her field, Cow was having trouble sleeping. She felt lonely now that her friends were so angry with her.

Perhaps she should have been more thoughtful. She would go and say sorry, even though it was late. And she'd be very careful not to ring her bell so loudly.

As she neared the barn, she heard the sound of her friends' voices.

"What are they shouting for?" she thought.

Suddenly, Cow could smell the smoke and ran for the barn as fast as her legs could carry her – her bell rang out loud and clear.

Clang! Clang! Clang!

The noise woke up the farmer and his wife.

They rushed outside and sprayed the barn with water – at last, the fire was out!

The next morning, the animals at Goosefeather Farm were in a very happy mood. Cow's bell had saved the day and they were very grateful!

"I was *so* glad to hear Cow's bell," said Horse.

"It was lucky that it rang so loud," added Cat.

"It's not such a terrible noise after all," said Hen. "Is it, everyone?"

Cow danced round in a circle, happily.

Ding-dong! Ding-dong!

"Well," repeated Hen. "Is it so bad?"

"Yes!" laughed everyone.